DIANA LILLIE
665-3490 - 664-8496

FOCUS ON SAFETY

Hazards at HOME

BILL GUTMAN

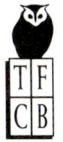

TFCB
Twenty-First Century Books
A Division of Henry Holt and Company/New York

For Cathy

Twenty-First Century Books
A Division of Henry Holt and Company, Inc.
115 West 18th Street
New York, NY 10011

Henry Holt® and colophon are trademarks of
Henry Holt and Company, Inc.
Publishers since 1866

Text copyright © 1996 by Bill Gutman
All rights reserved.
Published in Canada by Fitzhenry & Whiteside Ltd.
195 Allstate Parkway, Markham, Ontario L3R 4T8

Library of Congress Cataloging-in-Publication Data
Gutman, Bill.
Hazards at home / Bill Gutman.—1st ed.
p. cm.—(Focus on safety)
Summary: Describes potential dangers in the home, explains
how to prevent accidents, and advises what to do if one occurs.
1. Children's accidents—Prevention—Juvenile literature.
2. Home accidents—Prevention—Juvenile literature.
3. Safety education—Juvenile literature. [1. Safety.] I. Title. II.
Series: Gutman, Bill. Focus on safety.
HV675.72.G87 1996
613.6—dc20   95-34443
                                                                                      CIP
                                                                                      AC

ISBN 0-8050-4141-9
First Edition 1996

Printed in the United States of America
All first editions are printed on acid-free paper ∞.

10 9 8 7 6 5 4 3 2 1

Photo credits appear on page 80.

CONTENTS

FOREWORD		5
INTRODUCTION		7
ONE	FALLS	10
TWO	FIRES AND BURNS	19
THREE	POISONS	35
FOUR	FIREARMS	48
FIVE	SWIMMING POOLS AND OTHER DROWNING DANGERS	53
SIX	TOOLS AND MACHINERY	59
SEVEN	HOW TO HELP IF THERE IS AN ACCIDENT	70
FURTHER READING		77
ORGANIZATIONS TO CONTACT		78
INDEX		79

FOREWORD

Safety is a simple, six-letter word that means being secure and protected from harm. Everyone would like to feel safe, every day of their lives. That would be an ideal situation.

Unfortunately, none of us lives in a perfect world. In reality, this is a world where there are risks and where accidents and other bad things happen. And they can happen anywhere and at any time.

Many of the things that put us in jeopardy, however, can be avoided if we become more aware of our surroundings. All of us must be able to identify conditions that may put us in danger and take measures to alter those conditions. In other words, we must practice prevention.

For an overall focus on safety to really work, it must become a way of life, something each person is aware of every day. The safety net must always be up. No one wants to become just another statistic. And we should be willing to do everything in our power to keep that from happening.

INTRODUCTION

To many people, home has a special meaning—it is a safe haven. Home is a place where people escape everyday pressures and relax.

How many times have you come home, flopped onto your bed or sat down on your favorite chair, and just chilled out? Not a worry in the world. Not while you're home. Sure, chores and homework can be a drag, but everyone has to do them at some time. When you're finished, you can always hit the fridge for a snack or take a hot shower and then take it easy.

But there is a side to being home that not many people think about, not unless they have experienced it firsthand. Simply said, your home can be a booby trap. It can be a place where accidents are just waiting to happen: a danger zone where you have to tread lightly and carefully. Home accidents occur a lot more often than you might think, and many of them can be serious. Some are even life threatening.

The statistics are eye-opening. First of all, accidents in the home are the nation's second leading cause of accidental death. That's something to think about right there. Each year, according to the National Safety Council (NSC), approximately 22,500 people will die in home accidents. That's more fatalities than occur in work-related accidents. Only motor-vehicle accidents claim more lives each year.

Let's break it down. According to NSC statistics compiled in

1993, someone is injured in a home accident every five seconds! And someone dies as the result of a home accident every twenty-seven minutes. A "National Health Interview Survey" indicates that a total of 18,902,000 home injuries occurred in 1992 (the last year the survey was taken). This means that about 1 person in 13 suffered a home injury that required medical attention. And the NSC has said, flat out, that there is no more dangerous place than your own home.

There is some good news, though. The numbers have been declining. Between 1912 and 1993, accidental home-injury deaths per 100,000 population were reduced 68 percent, from 28 to 9. Going back to 1912, an estimated 27,000 persons were killed in home accidents. But there were just 21 million homes in the United States in 1912. By 1993 there were 96 million homes in America and the population had more than doubled. Deaths were down to 22,500. While 22,500 deaths represents a reduction, it's still far too many.

The kinds of accidents that can happen in your home are numerous—falls, fires, poisonings, accidents with tools and

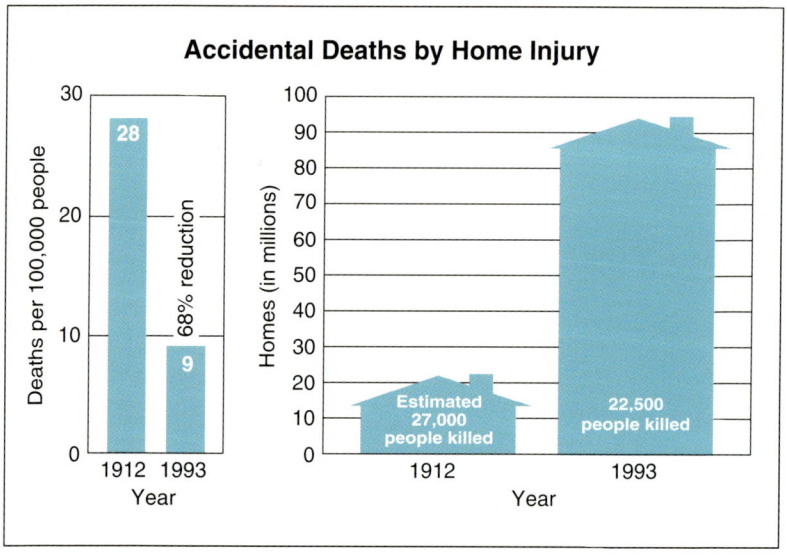

appliances, electric shock, drownings, and accidents with firearms. All of us are at risk, though it is the very young and very old who are most susceptible. Even the strongest, healthiest, and fittest of us can have an accident at home, especially if the risk factors are high.

What, then, can we do to try to change the statistics relating to home accidents? Two words that people often take for granted and even ignore are *be careful*. Being careful, however, *is* a good starting point. The most important element in home safety is prevention. Many accidents are preventable if the factors that lead to them are eliminated. Accident prevention is something that must be worked at every single day, and it is something you and your family can accomplish if you focus on safety and work together as a team.

There are, of course, some accidents that simply cannot be prevented. These freak accidents may be the result of nature, suddenly causing its own brand of destruction, or an accident that occurs because of just the right combination of natural forces. When these accidents occur, those at the scene must not panic. To help they must know immediately what to do.

Being "safe at home" is more than an expression used in a baseball game. It's something that each and every one of us must make a priority. Only then can your home be that safe haven you and your family want it to be.

FALLS

Whenever moviemakers want to have someone fall down a flight of stairs, they usually create a scene taking place at night. The character who will take the fall comes down a darkened hallway to the top of the stairs. Then the camera focuses on a roller skate or some other object that was left on the stairs. Everyone watching knows just what will happen next.

As soon as the "victim" starts down the stairs, he steps directly onto the object and boom . . . down he goes, usually head over heels. Because everyone watching the film knows what is going to happen, this kind of scene often causes great laughter. But, in real life, the situation is not so humorous. Thousands of people have fallen down flights of stairs after stepping on an unseen object left carelessly in their path.

Unless you are a professional stuntman, you don't want to fall down a flight of stairs. Absolutely nothing good can come of it. At best, you may wind up with some painful bruises. At worst, you can break a limb, you can possibly suffer a neck or spinal injury that can result in paralysis, or you can be killed. Once again, the statistics tell a grim story.

Nearly one out of every three home accidents is a fall of some kind. Falls down stairways alone account for 1.7 million serious injuries each year. More than 7,000 people are killed in accidental falls at home each year. A fall needn't involve a flight of stairs. There are falls from windows, falls off roofs and ladders, and even falls out of one's own bed. A fall in the bathtub can be one of the most dangerous of all.

Surprisingly, one of four falls happens on a level surface. People can be simply walking in their house or yard when they trip, or stumble, or fall over an object. By now you're probably wondering how so many people can be so clumsy.

Remember, all it takes is a split second. Just one misstep, one slight error in judgment, one object that's unseen in the night, or one shove while horsing around can cause a fall.

What can you do to prevent yourself and others from taking a bad fall in the "safety" of your own home? *Watch your step* would seem to be the best advice. But people can't step lightly every minute of the day and night. Everyone has to hurry once in a while and that's a prime time for accidents to happen. Therefore, other preventive measures should be taken. The more you and your family do to try to eliminate the possibility of an accident, the safer you will be.

STAIRS: THE NUMBER ONE CULPRIT

There is little doubt that stairways are the most dangerous area in the home. The American Association of Retired Persons (AARP), which focuses on the needs of the elderly, has called stairs "the most hazardous consumer product in the United States." Some 750,000 people are taken to emergency rooms each year because of falls on stairways.

Unfortunately, nothing is going to completely eliminate falls down stairways. Every now and then, someone will become dizzy on the stairs and fall. Or they will literally trip over their own feet. Sometimes a misstep just happens. But there *are* measures you can take to eliminate many unnecessary and dangerous falls:

1. Always make sure there are no objects of any kind left on the stairs. It doesn't have to be the proverbial roller skate that causes

If you keep the stairways in your house free of clutter, you may save someone in your family from a trip to the emergency room.

a fall. A book, a pile of clean towels, or any kind of toy can present a hazard.
2. No one can see in the dark. At night, light the stairway before you start down. Or leave a night-light on. Otherwise, you simply can't see your way clearly down the stairs.
3. If the stairs are not carpeted, make sure you are wearing shoes that give you traction. Walking down uncarpeted stairs in stocking feet can cause a fall. A rubber runner is a great covering for basement stairs that get a lot of traffic.
4. Never place a slippery throw rug at the top of the stairs. If you do, you may fall before you even take that first step.
5. Worn-out carpeting can also be a hazard because it can be slippery, even if you are wearing shoes.
6. A staircase should always have a handrail, and it should be secure, not loose and shaky.
7. Take one step at a time, both going up and going down. While more falls occur on the way down, people have been known to fall "up" the stairs.
8. If there are very young children in your family, or an elderly person who has difficulty walking, perhaps a gate or similar barrier should be placed at the top of the stairs. This may be a minor annoyance to the rest of the family, but it could prevent a catastrophe. And if you're in a hurry, remember not to jump the gate to save time. Slow down, just to be on the safe side.

OTHER POTENTIAL DANGERS

Most of us, in our right minds, are not going to fall out of a window. That seems like something that happens only to small children. Toddlers can be protected, however, by special window guards, which are required by law in some areas.

But here's another possible situation. Your best friend says, "Later," and leaves. Suddenly, you remember something you forgot to tell him. You open an upstairs window and holler to him.

He continues walking as you shout the message. He can't quite hear you. You lean a little farther out the window while you're still trying to get his attention. Then a little farther, then . . .

Ladders also present the potential for nasty falls. First of all, if heights and ladders make you nervous, get someone else to do the climbing. Even if you have no problem with heights, a shaky ladder can make *you* shaky. In fact, it's always a good idea to have someone spotting below, holding the ladder to reduce the wobble, and keeping the foot of the ladder from slipping. And if you are on a ladder, say cleaning a gutter, don't lean over to reach that extra inch farther. Use your head. Get down, move the ladder, and stay safe.

If you need to reach something on a high shelf, never climb up on a pile of objects. Don't put three or four books on a chair and then a small wooden box on top of the books. This sort of makeshift stepladder can lead to a disastrous fall.

In a recent movie about a comedian, he tells a joke about his daughter. He says that she kept complaining about having a headache in the morning. The punch line to the joke went like this: "I keep telling you when you get out of bed, get out *feet* first!"

If someone in your household has the potential to fall out of bed because of age or illness, a protective railing will help to keep the person safe. If you ever fall out of bed because of dizziness or some other feeling, tell your parents or guardians. And remember not to fool around on the top of a set of bunkbeds. A fall from a bed may not have the injury potential of other falls, but should still be avoided whenever possible.

Don't forget to be careful in the bathtub. A bathtub fall can be sudden and devastating. If your feet go out from under you, there is only a small, hard surface with edges on which to land. Metal knobs and faucets present a danger, too. Serious head injuries as well as broken bones can result from falls in a tub. Many of these injuries can be avoided simply by putting a rubber mat in the tub. The mat should have suction cups

Bunkbeds are found in many homes in America. Special care should be taken to prevent falls from the top bunk.

THE NATIONAL SAFETY COUNCIL

The National Safety Council, founded in 1913, is the primary source of safety and health information in the United States. Through its programs, the council tries to educate and influence American society to adopt and practice a variety of safety and good health policies.

The NSC was officially named a not-for-profit corporation by an Act of Congress in 1953. That meant the council could simply watch out for the health and safety of the public without contributing to or supporting any political party or candidate.

There are currently more than seventy chapters and affiliates of the NSC operating in the United States and Canada. These chapters support the council's ideas and services at the grassroots level. They serve as community contacts between people, local organizations, and the NSC, headquartered in Chicago, Illinois. Regional managers located in several U.S. cities can help each area of the country determine its safety and health needs.

underneath so it doesn't move. And it should be large enough to cover most of the stepping surface. In homes where a senior citizen is part of the family, safety railings can be installed on the side of the tub. Also, soft rubber covers for faucets are available to lessen the chance of injury if a fall does occur.

KEEP YOUR SAFETY NET UP

It's almost impossible to talk about every single situation that can cause a fall. Unanchored throw rugs can cause a fall at any time. A throw rug should have a nonskid backing or a nonskid pad under it. Two-sided carpet tape can also help to hold a

In addition, there are more than 18,500 businesses, labor organizations, schools, public agencies, private groups, and individuals who are members of the National Safety Council. Together, these organizations employ more than 30 million people.

The NSC produces booklets, manuals, newsletters, and safety bulletins dealing with such home safety and health concerns as falls, fire prevention, electrical hazards, and exercise and fitness. There are also materials that discuss recreational safety and health, bicycle safety, yard safety, swimming and boating safety, and the safety and health problems specific to each season.

This just scratches the surface of the things the National Safety Council does. Most of the injury statistics provided in this book were compiled by the NSC in their booklet *Accident Facts*. NSC information can easily be obtained by contacting the council at the address given at the back of this book.

throw rug firmly in place. Take a look around your house, and let your parents or guardians know if you find any rugs that need to be secured.

Clutter and mess anywhere can make conditions ripe for a fall. Always pick up after yourself and, if necessary, after others. It may seem like a drag to pick up your little brother's toys, but that's another easy thing that *you* can do to make your home a safer place.

If you and your family live where the winters are cold, there are going to be snowy, icy conditions from time to time. It takes just a split second for a person's feet to slip on pure ice. It's similar to a bathtub fall. The result can be a head injury, broken bones, bad bruises, or some combination of the three. Rarely does a person emerge from a fall on ice without an injury of some kind.

Always make sure your household has some salt, sand, or other substance on hand that will either melt ice or make it safe to walk across. If a winter storm is forecast and you have no sand or salt, remind an adult in your family to pick some up at the store. If there is a sudden storm and you don't have time to prepare, then walk across icy areas slowly, with very small steps, leaning forward slightly.

According to the National Safety Council, falls are the number one cause of accidental death in American homes. But, as this chapter has clearly shown, there are a number of easy things you can do to protect yourself and your family from dangerous falls.

FIRES AND BURNS

There is probably no more frightening feeling than to wake up in the middle of the night to find your room filling up with smoke or to see flames coming from a ceiling or hallway. A house or apartment fire can turn deadly in just a matter of minutes. Even if a fire doesn't take your life, it can rob you of your home and all your worldly possessions. Fires are now the third leading cause of accidental death in the home.

Fire can do more than kill people and destroy property and possessions. Burns are an extremely painful and dangerous injury. Even a small burn from a match or a red-hot pipe will hurt and throb for a period of time. Severe burns can leave terrible physical scars, as well as emotional ones. They cause skin, tissue, and nerve damage. The recovery period is often long and difficult. Many surgeries may be needed for skin grafting and other cosmetic repairs.

This is scary stuff. No one wants to be caught in a bad fire. Yet many fires are preventable. They are often the result of neglect, laziness, indifference, or carelessness. Perhaps people who have never been victims of a fire feel it can't happen to them. But it can happen to anyone. Once again, you and your family can work together to lower the odds of a fire taking place in your home.

Let's take a quick look at the statistics. The National Fire Protection Association (NFPA) says that there are about

520,000 home fires a year. These fires result in about 3,200 deaths and 21,500 serious injuries. That breaks down to a fire striking an American home every minute of every hour of every day! Think about it. Every minute while you're at school, playing with your friends, listening to music, taking a shower, or even sleeping, someone's home in the United States is catching fire.

What's more, eight out of every ten deaths from fire occur in fires at home. These statistics include deaths from both burns and suffocation, when smoke and fumes cut off a person's supply of oxygen. The most frequent victims of fire are young children and the elderly. They have the most difficulty escaping from fire situations. The highest number of fire-related deaths occur to people seventy-five years of age and older. Next, however, come youngsters up to the age of four.

About one-third of all deaths from fire happen between midnight and 4 A.M., when most families are sleeping. People in a burning home may wake up, but not be alert enough to get out. In addition, by the time the residents awaken, the fire may have already taken a firm hold on the house, creating smoke and poisonous gases. That combination can make it more difficult to escape.

These are sobering facts and figures. Fire should never be taken lightly.

CAUSES AND PREVENTION

Just as there are several different elements that can cause a fire, there are also many things that can be done to prevent one. It is important for everyone in your household to have a high level of fire safety awareness. While certain situations are more likely to result in a fire than others, you should learn about all of them.

There are several ways that the forces of nature can start a fire. One of them is lightning. Lightning bolts light up the sky

A fire in their home can be devastating to a family.

during violent thunderstorms, and claps of thunder make it seem as if the world might be coming to an end.

These storms can be dangerous. Torrential rains can cause flash floods and lightning strikes can knock trees across roads and onto power lines. That can result in power outages. But lightning also has the capacity to set a building on fire.

Lightning is really a huge electric spark. It builds up inside a thundercloud and then jumps outward. It can jump from cloud to cloud, or it can jump from a cloud to the ground. This is when it becomes most dangerous. Lightning can strike an object with tremendous voltage. It can electrocute or badly injure a person. Because it generates heat and sparks, lightning is capable of starting a fire.

Lightning usually seeks the highest point or tallest object in an area. For this reason, hilltop houses should be protected with some kind of lightning arrester, often called a lightning rod. This is usually a metal rod or system of wires that will catch the lightning first and divert the charge harmlessly into the ground. Always remain aware during a severe storm. If lightning strikes your home, you may have to react quickly to put out a fire.

Brush fires are another danger to homes in some areas. These fires usually occur in warm climates during periods of drought. California and the Pacific Northwest are just two areas where brush fires can often occur. They may be started by lightning or by careless people. When they occur in hilly or mountainous terrain, brush fires can be very difficult to control. This is especially true in dry, windy conditions.

If your home is in an area where brush fires happen, you may feel powerless against them. But there *is* something you can do. You and your family can create a firebreak around your home. A firebreak is an area that has been cleared of anything that might fuel a fire. Remove any trees or bushes that are close to your house. Otherwise, it may be easy for a wind-driven brush fire to continue right up to your home, then engulf it.

AN OUNCE OF PREVENTION

Here are a few random scenes that may have happened in your home or apartment:

- Mom and Dad go out and leave a half-empty pack of cigarettes behind. They won't miss one or two of them.
  How many youngsters have decided to try smoking cigarettes that way? How many have been caught—or nearly caught—in the basement, out in the barn, in their own room? And how many have had to dispose of that cigarette quickly by dabbing it out and throwing it in the wastebasket, tossing it out the window, or chucking it into a bucket?

- One of your friends gets hold of a bunch of fireworks. No one else is home, so you decide to set off a firecracker in the basement to see how loud it is. Or maybe you put a cardboard box over one and see how it muffles the sound. How much light will one or two sparklers give off if you burn them in your room at night?

- How many families have moved into a house and fallen in love with the fireplace in the living room or den? A warm, crackling fire is lovely on a winter night. But no one wants to clean the chimney—that's hard work and messy. And it's expensive to hire a chimney sweep. Would it be so terrible if the chimney isn't cleaned until next year?

- There's a chilly room in your drafty old house. The one radiator isn't making it warm enough. Someone gives your dad an electric space heater. But you've already got a television, stereo, lamps, computer, and some other things occupying the few electrical outlets in the room. No problem, your father says. He puts a second three-way receptacle into the wall socket and adds the heater to the mix.

By now it should be pretty obvious what all these situations have in common. They are examples of the kind of human carelessness that starts fires and costs lives. Cigarettes, fireworks, clogged chimneys, and overloaded electrical circuits are just some of the ways countless fires have started. It's the responsi-

Young people experimenting with cigarettes often fear getting caught. That can lead them to dispose of a lit cigarette carelessly, which may cause a fire.

bility of everyone in your family—adults and children alike—to make sure this doesn't happen in *your* home.

Careless smoking is the number one cause of home fires. It would be great if you could convince family members to quit smoking. But if you can't accomplish that, at the very least, you must insist that they smoke safely. It may be your life, as well as theirs, that's at stake.

Ask all the smokers in your household to remember these rules, for safety's sake:

1. No one should ever smoke in bed. Nor should they smoke when sleepy or drowsy, especially if they are sitting on a sofa or easy chair with lots of padding that can easily be set aflame by a spark or burning ash.
2. Lit cigarettes should not be balanced on the edge of a table or dresser, where they might be forgotten.
3. Burning cigarette butts should not be thrown out a window or left around dry grass or leaves in the yard.
4. Ashtrays that may still contain smoldering cigarette butts should never be emptied into a wastebasket or garbage can.

We won't spend much time discussing fireworks here. They are illegal in many states, and if you have them, you're breaking the law. Besides having the potential to start a fire in a great variety of ways, fireworks can cause severe injuries, including the loss of a hand or an eye. Leave the fireworks to the experts. If you enjoy a fireworks display, see a legal, organized showing, and stay safe.

Chimneys serving fireplaces or woodstoves should be cleaned regularly. Otherwise, a chimney fire is a real possibility. The culprit is creosote. Creosote is a highly flammable, black oily substance that is produced during the burning of wood. It can build up on the inside of a chimney. When conditions are right, it can burst into flames. If you're lucky, the flames will stay confined to the chimney and burn themselves out. But they can also spread to the rest of the house.

If you have a chimney fire, there are just a few things you can do. Special chimney fire extinguishers are available. Suggest that your parents or guardians buy one, and keep it handy. If you don't have an extinguisher, and you have an airtight wood-burning stove, shut it down. This will cut off the oxygen supply going up the chimney and help extinguish the fire faster. If you have an open fireplace, you might try to put out the remaining fire in the fireplace. Then call the fire department and leave the house immediately.

A creosote-fueled fire in a chimney will eventually burn itself out. But a crack in the chimney might allow the fire into the walls of the house. Burning cinders coming out of the chimney might land on the roof. So even if you feel a chimney fire has gone out, make sure the fire department comes and checks your house. This is very important.

Always remind your parents or guardians that chimneys should be cleaned before each cold season. Then they should be checked periodically. If creosote seems to be building up, the chimney may need to be cleaned during the wood-burning season as well.

Remember that space heater that was hooked into an already crowded wall socket? That might just be enough overload to cause an electrical fire. An overloaded socket can generate heat and/or sparking wires and start a fire in the wall. Wall fires are sometimes hard to locate and can spread quickly before the flames burst through.

Another fire hazard families need to be aware of is having long extension cords that are hidden under rugs. The cords can become frayed or shredded from being walked on. Once frayed, electrical cords are a fire hazard. Encourage the adults in your house to use as few extension cords as possible and never run them where they are walked on or can be tripped over.

FALSE ALARMS AND ARSON

Two of the biggest problems facing firefighters today are false alarms and arson. Both are crimes and both have the potential to cost lives. Don't ever let friends talk you into sending a false alarm or starting a little fire "just for the fun of it."

A false alarm is reporting a fire that doesn't exist. But the fire department has no way of knowing if an alarm is false. They will rush to the site of the reported fire. In doing so, there is always the chance that one of their trucks will be involved in a traffic accident. Someone can be hurt or killed.

In addition, there may be a real fire at the same time the firefighters are racing to a false alarm. It will take longer for the firefighters to get to the real fire. Every year, people die because firefighters who might have been able to save them were out chasing a false alarm.

Many false alarms are sent in by small children who do not understand the danger they are causing to others. Statistics show that one in five fire alarms is a false alarm. That's far too many.

Arson is when a person, called an arsonist, starts a fire on purpose. This is a very serious crime. If someone is killed in a fire started deliberately, the arsonist may be charged with murder. Some arsonists are mentally ill. They get a thrill from seeing a huge fire. They may keep setting fires until they are caught.

Kids will sometimes set a fire as a prank. They often don't realize that the fire can spread and result in loss of property, serious injury, and even death. What started as a "fun" prank then becomes a tragedy. And the prank becomes a crime.

Many homes today have what is commonly called an entertainment center. This large cabinet or shelving unit may hold a television, VCR, cable box, and a stereo with four or five parts. These appliances each have individual electrical cords. People tend to plug all of them into one double wall receptacle, using a combination of extension cords and three-way, add-on plugs.

Once again, an electrical overload is possible. If this situation exists in your home, be sure to tell your parents or guardians. If there is no second outlet within reach, your family will need to call a professional electrician for his suggestions. It may be that the living room or den needs additional outlets to handle the load. Or the electrician may suggest a multi-outlet power strip that automatically shuts off if there is an electrical overload.

You need to be aware that space heaters can be fire hazards in another way, too. Never use one to dry wet clothing. Any kind of space heater should be at least thirty-six inches away from walls, curtains, bedding, or anything that is flammable.

Heaters that use a flammable liquid such as kerosene are illegal in many apartment buildings. They should be used in private homes only with the utmost care. Only adults should light a kerosene heater, clean it, or fill it. They must follow all the manufacturer's suggestions to the letter. Many, many tragic fires have resulted from the improper use of kerosene heaters.

OTHER FIRE HAZARDS

Let's look at a few more potential fire hazards that can be avoided with care and family teamwork.

The kitchen is an obvious place to start. The stove, toaster oven, microwave, deep fryer, and other cooking appliances all can be the starting points of a fire. Whether you cook regularly or just once in a while, always be careful. Take special care when using cooking grease such as butter or oil. If grease should burst into flames, put a cover on the pot immediately to smother the fire. If no cover is available, use salt, baking soda, or a fire extinguisher. *Never* throw water on a grease fire. The hot grease may splash and spatter all over you.

Don't cook while wearing loose and baggy clothes that might come in contact with a red-hot burner or open flame. Baggy sleeves are especially dangerous. Not only might they contact a hot burner and burst into flames, but they can also catch on a pot handle, causing a bad spill of hot food or liquid.

Here are a few more hazards you and your family should be aware of:

1. Do not let rubbish accumulate in attics and basements, especially papers, rags, and old clothes. Attics can get very hot from the summer sun. Basements have furnaces and other heat sources. Either place could be a location where a fire might begin.
2. Flammable liquids, such as kerosene, gasoline, and paint thinner should be kept in tightly closed metal containers. And they should be kept far away from heat sources. They should never be kept in places where heat can become extreme.
3. Rags that have been used to wipe up oil or paint should be stored in metal containers with lids. They should never be left in a closet or with a pile of papers or other flammable material.
4. Do not leave matches or cigarette lighters where young children can reach them.
5. Always keep a close eye on gas appliances. If you have a gas stove, make sure the pilot lights stay lit. Propane torches, stoves, and gas grills should all be handled with care. Do not ignore even the slightest indication of a gas leak. If you smell gas, the gas company should be called immediately. If the odor of gas in your home is strong, call the gas company from another location. Gas is very explosive and can easily ignite from the smallest spark, even one created by your telephone.

6. Be careful with any small appliances that generate heat, such as hair dryers or curling irons. These appliances should be used carefully and *never* left on or even plugged in if you are not right there. The heat from a curling iron can give you a serious burn and the heat from a hair dryer has been known to cause aerosol cans to explode (if the can is in the direct path of the heat).

WHAT TO DO IF THERE IS A FIRE

Don't panic! That's definitely the first rule of dealing with any emergency situation. If you wake up at night and your house is on fire, it's hard to stay calm. It will be easier if you plan ahead. That means being prepared.

The two most important pieces of fire-related equipment to have in your home are smoke detectors and fire extinguishers. A smoke detector is indispensable. It will alert you and your family to a possible fire long before your own senses will.

Unfortunately, many people install smoke detectors and then forget about them. A smoke detector with a dead battery is useless. Batteries should be checked once a month (the detector has a test button that produces the alert sound) and changed at least once a year. Pick a date, maybe your own birthday, and make it your responsibility to change the battery in your detectors on that day.

The National Fire Protection Association strongly suggests putting a smoke detector outside each sleeping area and on each level of the home. That includes the basement. And if you sleep with the bedroom door closed, you might want a detector in your room, as well. The sooner you are alerted to the possibility of fire, the sooner you can act. Because smoke detectors can sense minute amounts of toxic gas before the odor is strong enough to wake the average person, they have saved countless lives.

Fire extinguishers provide a means to put a small fire out

before it can spread. Every family should keep several around the house, especially in the kitchen. There are different types of extinguishers. For instance, some will not put out grease fires. An all-purpose extinguisher that will handle all types of fires is probably best for your family. Ask your parents or guardians to show you how the extinguisher works. You may even want to practice a bit so you'll know exactly what to do if there is a fire.

PLAN YOUR ESCAPE

Many deaths and serious injuries occur in fires because people panic. The fire takes them by complete surprise and they have no clue about what to do. No one should ever assume that a sudden home fire will never happen to them. On the contrary, it's safer to assume that it *will* happen. Then, you can plan accordingly.

If you and your family have done your homework, a working smoke detector will alert you that there is a fire. You must then assess the situation quickly. First make sure that everyone else in the house is also alerted. Your next instinct may be to go after the fire extinguisher and try to put the fire out yourself.

Here's a quick rule of thumb. It is not recommended that an untrained person try to put out a fire that is larger than one in a wastebasket. So don't try to be a hero with a fire extinguisher if the fire is already large and spreading.

Get out quickly!

You and the rest of your family must follow your escape plan. This is something every family should have. It is important to know just what to do and to do it quickly. And it is essential to have home fire drills periodically. These escape drills will help even the youngest members of the family to remember what to do in case of a fire.

Here are a number of tips recommended by the NFPA in making an escape plan for your family:

A firefighter in full gear can be a scary sight to a young child. Make sure your younger brothers and sisters can recognize a rescuer in an emergency.

1. There should be two escape routes from each room, especially the bedrooms. If a second-floor window might be used in an escape, have a good rope ladder handy.
2. If you live in an apartment, be very familiar with all fire exits and fire escapes in your building.
3. Make sure everyone in the house knows how to quickly operate the locks on doors, windows, and window gates.
4. Never try to escape an apartment fire by using an elevator. There may be a power failure and you'll be stuck. In addition, fire may enter the elevator shaft. Use the stairs instead.
5. Close all doors behind you as you leave. It will slow the fire down. If you come upon a closed door and it feels hot to your hand, **do not open it**! The blaze may be right behind that door and the superheated air that goes with it can kill instantly.
6. If the house or room is already filling with smoke, crouch or crawl. The air near the floor is safer.
7. Pay special attention to young children. Have the windows of their rooms marked with "Tot-Finder" decals to show firefighters the location. These decals are available at many local firehouses.
8. Show young children pictures of firefighters in their full gear. That way, they won't be frightened and run or hide if a firefighter comes to rescue them.
9. Everyone, including young children, should know how to "stop, drop, and roll" if their clothing catches fire. That means stop running, drop to the ground, cover your face with your hands, and roll back and forth on the ground until the fire is out.
10. Contact the fire department as soon as possible after exiting the burning building. Pull the fire-alarm box if there is one, or dial 911. If your town does not have a 911 system, call the operator to report the fire. The operator will connect you with the fire department.
11. Your family escape plan should include a spot outside the burning building where everyone meets once they are out. That way, you'll know quickly if one of your family members is missing.

SCALDING BURNS

At the end of an active, busy day you look forward to a relaxing hot shower. As you enter the shower you're thinking about that touchdown you scored in the football game, or the A you got on the big test. You forget to adjust the cold water and wind up stepping into red-hot water.

If the water is too hot, you can get a painful burn. Burns from very hot water or steam are called scalding burns. They can be very serious. In most homes, there is a way to adjust the temperature of the hot water. If you feel the water in your house is too hot before the cold is turned on, ask your parents or guardians to have the water temperature lowered.

The water should be just hot enough so that you need a little cold water for the shower or to wash your hands. But the hot water by itself should not be scalding. That's dangerous.

12. Once outside, *do not* go back inside the building for any reason. If there is someone still inside, tell a trained firefighter as soon as possible. Do not try to be a hero. You may not realize how bad the fire is or how weak the building's structure has become. Never go back inside a burning building to rescue a pet.

A great deal of time and planning should go into making your home safe from fire. Hopefully, by working together to prevent fires, you and your family can avoid ever having to face one.

POISONS

A poison is any substance that, in a large enough amount, can damage the body. Poisons can enter the body through the skin, mouth, or nose. Because there are many poisonous substances kept around the home, it is often easy to forget just how dangerous they can be.

Accidental poisoning remains the second leading cause of death in home accidents. National Safety Council statistics show that in 1993, there were 5,300 deaths from solid and liquid poisons, plus another 400 fatalities from gases and vapors, mainly carbon monoxide. That's even more fatalities than from fires.

While youngsters are always at risk of accidentally swallowing a harmful substance, the largest group of poisoning deaths occurs in persons between the ages of eighteen and forty-four. However, the percentage of fatalities is small compared to the total number of poisonings each year. The NSC estimates that there are two million nonfatal poisonings each year.

Surprisingly, the death rate from accidental poisonings is increasing. In 1960, there was an average of 0.9 deaths per 100,000 people. By 1990, it had doubled to 2.0 deaths per 100,000 people. The increase, however, is due primarily to accidental overdoses of drugs. That includes both prescription medications and illegal drugs.

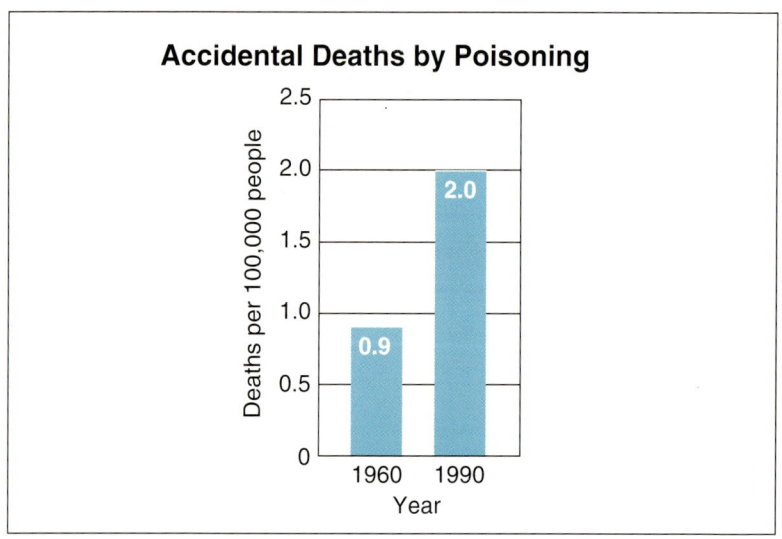

Liquid and solid poisons most commonly found in the home can be grouped into five different categories:

1. Pesticides and chemicals that are used to kill insects, rodents, and some plants.
2. Drugs or medicines that are safe when used properly but dangerous when taken in large amounts.
3. Caustic or burning chemicals. These are either acids or alkalis. Highly acidic substances include rust removers, metal polishes, and toilet bowl cleaners. Alkali substances include lye, drain cleaners, ammonia water, and many soaps and detergents.
4. Petroleum products, such as gasoline, kerosene, turpentine, paint thinner, and furniture polish.
5. Poisonous leaves or berries of plants such as English ivy, mistletoe, philodendron, dieffenbachia, holly, and poinsettia.

WHAT POISONS DO

Poisons can affect the body in several ways, none of them very pleasant. Caustic substances such as acids and strong alkalis

Many household cleaning products are poisonous. The skull and crossbones is an internationally recognized warning symbol for poison.

cause burns. They can burn the mouth, esophagus, and stomach. Other types of poisons act differently.

An overdose of sleeping tablets can affect the brain. This type of overdose causes the brain to stop controlling breathing. Then the lungs cannot take in enough oxygen and the result can be death. Some other medicines, such as antidepressants, can damage the heart if abused. Others can affect the liver. So even a medicine that can help people becomes a poison if it's abused.

Methanol, a form of alcohol found in antifreeze, affects the eyes and can cause blindness if swallowed. Carbon monoxide, a colorless, odorless gas, can kill in a different way. It attaches itself to red blood cells 250 times as fast as oxygen. This means it can capture red blood cells and keep them from carrying oxygen to all parts of the body. A victim of carbon monoxide poisoning dies from oxygen starvation.

WHO IS AT RISK?

Accidental poisoning can occur at any time. There are, of course, situations that pose a higher risk than others. Babies are always at risk because they like to put things in their mouths. This is especially true for liquids and medicines or other things in brightly colored packages.

There is one easy way you and your family can cut down the risk to very young children. Do not let them see anyone drink medicine from the bottle. They may imitate that behavior later, when no one is watching. Never tell a youngster that medicine is candy. It might seem like a good way to get the child to take her medicine, but it could backfire if she decides she wants more "candy," and takes some on her own.

Teenagers, as well as adults, can fall victim to another kind of risk. That is using either prescription medications or illegal drugs to deal with problems they feel are overwhelming. In many cases, they are not trying to harm or kill themselves. But the misuse of these substances can be deadly. Misuse can be in the form of an overdose. Or it can be the use of a combination of substances that react badly with each other.

Some people will use medications to try to alter their moods, to sleep, or even to stay awake. While these substances have *bona fide* medical uses, their misuse can easily lead to accidental poisoning.

There are also people who are allergic to certain medications. If you don't know you are allergic and take what is normally a safe drug, your body may react violently. You are, in effect, being poisoned. The antibiotic penicillin was once considered a wonder drug because it could stop so many illnesses. Yet people allergic to penicillin can have so violent a reaction that it can result in death. Many people are also allergic to aspirin and can have a bad reaction if they take it.

PREVENTING POISONING

The rules for avoiding accidental poisoning are actually very simple. The problem is getting people to follow them.

For starters, you and your family should keep all medications and other poisonous substances out of the reach of young children. Cabinets containing dangerous substances should be kept locked. Medicines should be kept in marked childproof containers. Unused medicines should be disposed of safely.

Statistics seem to show some improvement in this area of poison prevention. From 1961 to 1991, the last year detailed figures were available, the death rate by poison for children up to the age of four declined dramatically. In 1961, there were 2.2 deaths by poison in this age group per 100,000 persons. By 1991, there were only 0.3 deaths per 100,000. That's very encouraging.

Poisons should always be handled by adults. If your parents or guardians work with any poisonous substances, remind them to wash their hands immediately afterward. They should never

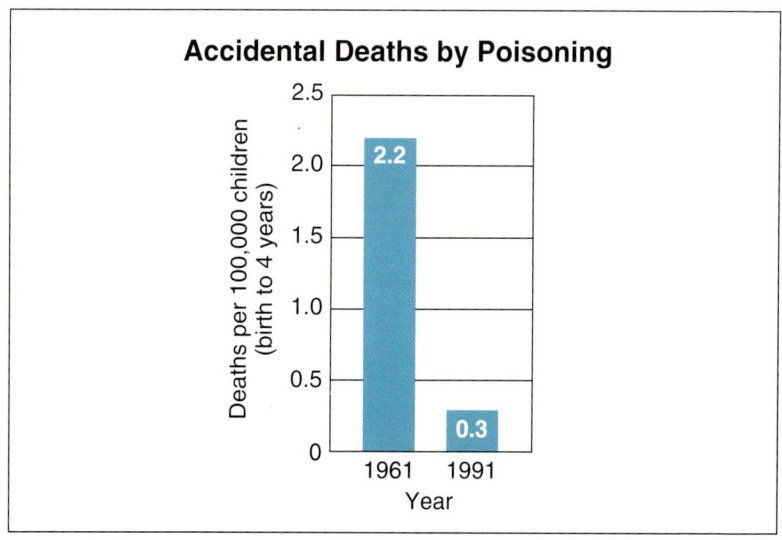

work with a poison near food. A poisonous substance should never be put in an unmarked container. It might be mistaken for something else. Nor should a poison ever be put into a container that originally contained a nonpoisonous substance. That, too, can lead to disaster.

Prescription drugs should also be handled with care. No one should ever take medicine intended for another person. If you take any medicine, even an aspirin, and begin to feel any kind of strange reaction, tell your parents or guardians immediately. They should call a doctor.

If you know of anyone in your household who is abusing any kind of drug, you may not be able to get them to stop or seek help. But you can try to make sure that the younger members of your family never have access to drugs that might poison them.

CARBON MONOXIDE

In September 1994, former tennis star Vitas Gerulaitis was found dead in a friend's home in Long Island, New York. At first it appeared he had died in his sleep. There was speculation that perhaps drugs or some other substance were involved. It was soon learned, however, that Gerulaitis had indeed died in his sleep. He was poisoned by carbon monoxide that had been released into the house by a faulty heater.

Because it is odorless and colorless, carbon monoxide is a very deadly poison. It can sneak up on a person without her realizing it. And it can kill quickly by starving the body of oxygen.

But carbon monoxide doesn't always kill. In 1992, a family rented a townhouse in Pittsburgh, Pennsylvania. There was a husband, wife, and two young girls, ages six and three. Shortly after moving in, the entire family began showing signs of illness—fatigue, headaches, nausea, and dizziness. The symptoms continued over a period of four months.

At first doctors suspected a form of flu and checked for various viruses. The youngest daughter lost nine pounds, and everyone in the family continued to feel ill. It wasn't until the older daughter returned from spending a few days at a friend's house that the riddle was solved. The older girl came back from the visit feeling fine, but within an hour of her return complained of feeling sick.

Experts checked the townhouse and found that the furnace had been releasing low levels of carbon monoxide. The gas was slowly poisoning the entire family. Fortunately, the problem was discovered in time and no lives were lost. The family recovered. It could have been a tragic accident, but this particular family was very lucky.

Carbon monoxide is always a by-product of combustion. Whenever a fuel such as coal, gasoline, wood, kerosene, or oil is burned, carbon monoxide is released. The exhaust of automobiles, buses, and trucks always releases the gas. People who warm up their cars in closed garages are in danger of poisoning themselves.

In fact, if you are in a car that is idling in traffic, always

POISON CONTROL CENTERS

Everyone should be very careful to prevent accidental poisoning. But if someone *is* poisoned accidentally, there is a nationwide network set up to give immediate help. There are more than 550 poison control centers in the United States alone.

These centers operate twenty-four hours a day, their phones manned by people who know what to do no matter what kind of poisoning has occurred. You can call poison control centers to get information about the poisonous substances in various products. The people working there can also tell you about the symptoms and treatment for different poisons.

In case of poisoning, the person at the poison control center will tell you what to do immediately. They will probably also sug-

A call to a poison control center will get you help immediately in case of an accidental poisoning.

make sure a window is open. You must have a source of fresh oxygen. That's why the Pittsburgh family didn't die. There was just enough oxygen in the house to keep the carbon monoxide below the danger level.

How can you tell if carbon monoxide is making you sick? The first symptom you may feel is a tightness around the forehead. Then a headache. You may also begin to feel dizzy and gest you call a doctor or even arrange to send an ambulance to your home. It's also possible they will suggest an antidote you can give the victim right away.

An antidote is a substance that will overcome the harmful effects of some poisons. Sometimes, antidotes are printed right on the labels of poisonous substances. This information is not 100 percent reliable. A medical expert or poison control center can suggest the best possible antidote.

An antidote can be anything from fresh air for a person who has inhaled poisonous fumes to something as simple as milk or water. There are other antidotes, as well, but it's best to get that information from a doctor or poison control center.

Find out the telephone number for the poison control center in your area. If there isn't one nearby, have your parents or guardians talk to local officials about starting one. Or perhaps you can find a poison control center in a nearby town or city. Record that number near every phone in the house, just in case you need help quickly in an emergency.

tired. Then your eyes may begin to blur. Next will come a feeling of nausea. If you or any member of your family feel these symptoms, get out into some fresh air immediately. Don't go back into the place where you felt the symptoms until it can be checked out.

There are several ways to prevent carbon monoxide poisoning. Keeping a window open in your family vehicle is just one.

Another is for your parents or guardian to make sure all burning appliances (gas stoves, furnaces, woodstoves) in your home are installed properly. They should then be cleaned and checked periodically.

Today there is an excellent way to keep safe from carbon monoxide poisoning. Your family can buy a carbon monoxide detector. These detectors are very similar to smoke detectors and sound an alarm as soon as they detect any amount of the deadly gas in the home. Make sure the detector your family buys is approved by the Underwriters' Laboratory. That way, you'll know the model has been tested and is a top-notch product.

OTHER POSSIBLE POISONS

There are several other airborne poisons that can threaten the health of the people in your household. Everyone should be aware of these poisons and what they can do if undetected.

The first is radon, a colorless and odorless radioactive gas. It is formed by the breakdown of natural uranium in rocks and soil. In the open air, radon poses no danger to people. But if it seeps into homes, it can build to a harmful level. The Environmental Protection Agency (EPA) estimates that 55 percent of the radiation that people acquire over the course of their lives comes from breathing radon.

Radiation, of course, is very dangerous. Atomic weapons give off huge amounts of radiation. Nuclear power plants use radiation, which is kept trapped within the plant. Exposure to radiation can cause several types of cancer. In the case of radon, the EPA feels that the gas causes between 7,000 and 30,000 deaths each year from lung cancer in adults. This is the result of the accumulation of radiation caused by breathing radon over many years.

Radon can enter homes through ground-level openings such as pipes, drains, and cracks in the foundation. It can even be dispersed by well water, which can absorb it underground and disperse it into the air through showers and faucets. There are now inexpensive radon test kits, which indicate the amount of radon in a home. A private contractor can also come in and do the testing for your family.

If your home contains radon, basement drains, pipes, and sumps need to be covered and sealed. Cracks in the foundation should also be sealed and then the house should be tested again. A contractor can also install a venting pipe that will draw radon from beneath the house and disperse it harmlessly into the air.

Radon doesn't pose the same kind of immediate threat as carbon monoxide. But over a long period of time, it can be a danger that will catch up with you and your family in later years.

Another potential source of poison in the home is formaldehyde. Formaldehyde is a colorless but pungent gas that is used in liquid solution as a disinfectant and preservative. It is also used in building materials such as particleboard, plywood, and paneling. The gas can seep out slowly from these materials over a period of a year or two.

Not everyone is sensitive to low levels of formaldehyde. But if you, or any member of your household are, you might begin to experience itchy, dry eyes or throat, coughing, and nausea. If you are spending time in a room that has been redone recently and have these symptoms, you might ask your parents or guardians to check the building materials to see if they contain formaldehyde.

Lead has been a source of home contamination for many years. In fact, there is probably less of it now than in years past because not as many products are made using lead today. Children between the ages of six months and six years who live or go to school or day care in old buildings are at the highest risk for lead poisoning.

Though lead-based paint was banned in the United States in 1977, it remains on the walls and woodwork in some fifty-

Homeowners can test for radon themselves, or they can hire a contractor to test for the odorless, colorless gas.

seven million homes. The dust and chips from this paint are the leading cause of lead poisoning in children.

If the paint in a home is determined to be lead-based, it can be painted over with a non-lead paint. This will lessen the chance of lead poisoning, since only the chips and dust of the underlying lead-based paint would cause a problem.

Young children absorb lead five times faster than adults. In small doses, it can slow physical and mental development. Higher doses can cause diarrhea, vomiting, headaches, difficulty walking and, in some cases, death. If a young child in your household shows symptoms of lead poisoning, your parents or guardians should take her to a doctor immediately. It is also a good idea to feed children foods containing iron and calcium. Both of these substances can reduce the amount of lead absorbed by the body.

FIREARMS

There is perhaps nothing more tragic than a life lost in a firearms accident, especially when it involves a young child. Yet there have been countless such cases. Either the children were too young to realize what might happen or someone assumed a gun wasn't loaded, and it was.

That kind of mistake can not only end a life, but can deeply affect all those associated with the accident. Think about it. There is the person who pulled the trigger, the person who owned the gun but failed to keep it secure, as well as the families of both parties. All, in a sense, become victims.

These senseless accidents continue to happen in homes all over the country. In New Jersey recently, a nine-year-old boy accidentally shot his seven-year-old sister to death. This tragedy will live with the entire family for the rest of their lives. Clearly, having a firearm in the home brings with it a huge responsibility.

While the total number of accidental deaths caused by firearms in the home doesn't approach those caused by falls, fires, and poisonings, these deaths cannot be ignored. In 1992, the National Safety Council estimated the number of deaths from home firearm accidents at eight hundred per year. This total has been the same since 1986. It has come down from a high of fourteen hundred in 1970 and 1974. So things are getting better, but not fast enough.

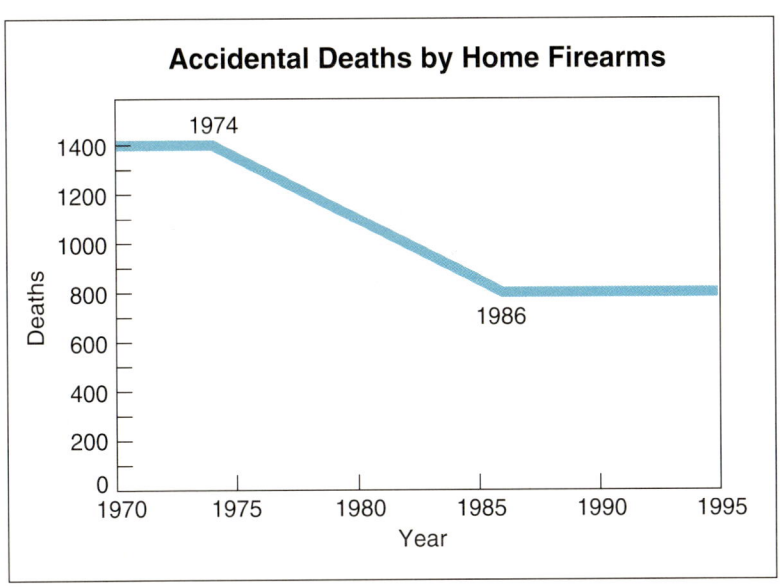

The NSC also estimates that for every death, there are at least five nonfatal gunshot injuries. So nearly five thousand people are killed or injured by firearms at home each year. The fifteen to twenty-four-year-old age group has the largest number of fatalities. In addition, half of all children under sixteen who are injured in a handgun accident are shot in their own home.

The remedy to all this seems simple. No gun in the house; no accidents. Unfortunately, that is an unrealistic goal that is never going to be achieved. People keep firearms for various reasons. Some like to hunt. Others enjoy target shooting. Still others are collectors. Law enforcement officers are required to have guns. And many people today feel that they need a gun in the house to protect their property and family.

So there are always going to be guns in homes. The only hope of reducing the number of injuries and fatalities even more will be to eliminate all traces of carelessness and to educate children about gun safety from a very young age.

What would you do, for example, if you found a handgun

Children need to be educated about gun safety from an early age. Firearms in the home can be the cause of needless tragedy.

lying on your kitchen table? Do not pick it up and examine it. Do not look down the barrel. Do not aim it and pull the trigger. Do not rush to show it to a friend or to your little brother. But do not ignore it, especially if you have younger brothers and sisters at home.

If the owner of the gun is in the house, call that person immediately. Tell him to put the gun away safely. But if no responsible adult is home, and there are younger children in the house, get everyone out of the room where the gun is. Telephone an adult relative or friend. Ask him or her to come immediately and take charge of the situation.

Obviously, guns in the home should be kept in a locked cabinet, box, or drawer. In fact, as an extra safety measure, guns can also have a trigger lock. That prevents anyone from accidentally pulling the trigger.

Guns in the home should never be left loaded. The ammunition should be locked away in a separate place. These are hard and fast rules that should *always* be followed. If there is a gun owner in your household who is not following these rules, talk to him. You can admit that you fear for your own safety and that of your entire family. Loaded guns left out in the open can injure and kill.

Parents or guardians should make sure young children understand the difference between a toy gun and the real thing. In addition, they should stress that no one should ever point a toy gun at a stranger. That person could mistake the toy gun for a real gun. If the stranger has a firearm, he might shoot in response.

Older children and other members of the family should always be taught the rules for safe handling of firearms. Young children should be taught never to touch them, no matter what the situation.

LEARNING TO HANDLE FIREARMS SAFELY

There will always be guns in some homes in the United States. If guns are going to be kept in the home, it may be a good idea for older children to learn about the safe handling of weapons.

Of course, an adult who is familiar with guns can teach the children how to handle them. But children may develop even more respect for the power of a firearm if they learn in an organized program with others.

There are probably a number of organizations in your town that teach the safe handling of firearms. Some of these might be shooting ranges, rod and gun clubs, hunting organizations, or the National Rifle Association, which may have a chapter in your area. Some law enforcement agencies may also offer safe firearm instruction.

Certified instructors often teach young people how to handle firearms safely.

If there are guns kept in your home and you feel you must know more about them, speak to your parents or guardians. If you feel you want to learn about how to handle firearms for the sake of safety and confidence, tell the gun owners just how you feel.

5
SWIMMING POOLS AND OTHER DROWNING DANGERS

Drowning at home is a form of accident that can often be prevented. Yet according to the National Safety Council, some eight hundred people a year drown in home accidents, in swimming pools, hot tubs, and even in bathtubs. These statistics do not include drownings from floods and other natural disasters.

Young children up to the age of four are the most likely drowning victims simply because most of them can't swim. The only other age group with a significant number of drowning fatalities are those seventy-five years of age and older. Once again, a little preventive care and strict adherence to a few basic rules could eliminate most of these tragedies.

If you and your family have an aboveground pool, the entire family should be taught never to leave the ladder in the pool when a swimmer is not there. Children as young as toddlers may find a way to climb the ladder and fall into the pool. Even when the pool is covered, the ladder should be removed, just to be on the safe side.

The best way for your family to keep a child from getting into the pool is to construct a fence around the pool area. A fence around in-ground pools is required by law in many areas. The gate in the fence should have a lock, and the lock should be high enough so young children can't reach it.

It might also be wise for your family to invest in a floating alarm. This is a motion-detector alarm that floats on the sur-

Remember to be safety conscious if you have a pool at home. Backyard pools have no lifeguards, but even so, safe swimming rules should be followed.

face of the water and will sound if someone falls or jumps into the pool.

Where bathtubs are concerned, the safety rule is clear. Simply stay with any infant or toddler while she is in the tub. In just the time it takes to answer a phone call, a child may slip below the surface of the water and panic. Children should never be left alone in pools. They may be floating in a tube or on an inflated pillow, but it only takes a split second for a tragedy to occur.

Don't assume a child is safe just because she is in a wading pool. There is more than enough water for a tragedy to occur. When there are young children in a family, they must always be protected from the threat water presents.

Even the household toilet is a potential danger. Young children, especially toddlers, have been known to drown in toilets when the lid was left up. They lean in out of curiosity, and they don't have the strength to pull their heads back out. It is wise to put lid locks on all toilets in houses where young children live. (These are inexpensive devices that can be purchased in many discount and department stores.)

BASIC POOL RULES

If you have a backyard swimming pool, in ground or aboveground, make sure you, your family, and your friends observe these safety rules:

1. There should be no horsing around in the water, no wrestling or other forms of roughhousing. No chicken fights where one person sits on the shoulders of another and tries to knock her opponent off the shoulders of another person should be allowed. Someone could fall and hit her head on the side of the pool.
2. There should be absolutely no diving into an aboveground pool that is four feet deep or less. Diving into a shallow aboveground

YOU'RE NEVER TOO YOUNG TO SWIM

Unless they have already had a bad experience, infants and toddlers do not normally have a fear of the water. They will instinctively hold their breath underwater. And because they do not fear the water, they can sense the natural buoyancy in their bodies. So they know they can stay on the surface.

As strange as it may seem, these very young children can often be taught to swim very quickly. There are many programs available in most towns and cities specifically geared to teach youngsters between the ages of six months and five years to swim. The American Red Cross, the YMCA and YWCA are just three of the groups that regularly sponsor these programs.

Children as young as six months can be taught to swim.

It isn't unusual to see a youngster, still too young to walk, paddling happily through the water, a big smile on her face. Youngsters often enjoy learning to swim. This is especially true if they are working with a parent. Having their mother and/or father with them gives them even more confidence in the water.

Many parents feel that by teaching their youngsters how to swim at a very early age they can not only give them confidence, but can cut down the odds of those youngsters falling victim to an accidental drowning. They feel that if a toddler who knows how to swim falls into a pool, she can stay afloat until help comes. And she won't have that panicky fear of water that has caused many unfortunate youngsters to drown.

But there is a down side to these early swimming programs that cannot be ignored. It is wise for anyone who decides to teach a very young child to swim to keep several things in mind:

1. Some infants will swallow water during these lessons. If an infant swallows too much, she can contract a condition called *water intoxication*. This condition disrupts the mineral balance in the infant's blood and can, in some cases, prove fatal. To guard against this condition, the American Red Cross does not allow youngsters to be submerged more than three times during a swim class.

2. Some people feel that even infants or toddlers who have learned to swim *will* panic if they are alone and accidentally fall into an unattended pool.

3. The ability to swim may attract the youngster to a pool or body of water and thereby *increase* the risk of an accident or, worse yet, a drowning.

Parents who teach youngsters to swim should be aware of all these factors. It would also be irresponsible for parents who teach their infants and toddlers to swim to turn them loose at a local swimming pool or beach. Many experts feel that children should not be allowed to swim on their own until they have good depth perception and the ability to use good judgment in dangerous situations.

So, be careful. If your infant brother or sister can already swim, that's great. Even so, never assume very young children can take care of themselves in the water. They still need to be carefully supervised.

pool or the shallow end of an in-ground pool can result in a head or neck injury.
3. There should be no dive bombing another person already in the pool. You may not judge the jump right and instead of landing alongside the person and splashing her, you might land on top of her. That can cause an injury to both the jumper and the person in the pool.
4. Under no circumstances should anyone be thrown into the pool against her wishes. This practice can also result in an injury.

Swimming at home should be fun and safe. Just be aware that the same rules of safety that apply to public pools or beaches should be observed at your family's pool.

6

TOOLS AND MACHINERY

Many people today are do-it-yourselfers. Some people enjoy working with their hands. Others find they can save money by doing certain projects around their home or apartment. Homeowners also save money by maintaining their house and property. Therefore, many households in the United States not only have heavy-duty electrical appliances, but a full array of power tools, as well. In addition, homeowners may have lawn mowers, electric hedge clippers, wood chippers, chain saws, rototillers, and other kinds of machinery for the yard.

Any one of these tools and appliances can cause an accident if it is not used and cared for properly. These types of accidents usually result in injuries much more often than death, but the injuries can be severe.

In fact, the number of estimated yearly injuries from home appliances, tools, and machinery is eye-opening. In a survey taken by the National Electronic Injury Surveillance System (NEISS) in 1991, injury statistics were recorded from a representative sampling of hospitals in the United States. The injury totals listed in Table 1 represent estimates of the number of cases treated in hospital emergency rooms nationwide that are associated with appliances, tools, and machinery.

TABLE 1

Workshop manual tools	118,799
Power home workshop saws, all	94,076
Lawn mowers, all types	76,133
Electric fixtures, lamps, equipment	55,191
Cooking ranges, ovens, et cetera	54,659
Lawn, garden care equipment	54,507
Chain saws	44,019
Sound recording, reproducing equipment	42,678
Miscellaneous workshop equipment	40,147
Hand garden tools	38,796
Television sets, stands	36,995
Refrigerators, freezers	31,741
Miscellaneous household appliances	30,532
Power home tools, except saws	29,014
Other power lawn equipment	19,424
Welding, soldering, cutting tools	19,368
Washers, dryers	19,205
Hatchets, axes	18,270
Barbecue grills, stoves, equipment	15,786
Trimmers, small power garden tools	11,525

The numbers are staggering. Maybe you're asking how nearly 37,000 people can be injured by a television or stand each year, or why more than 38,000 Americans needed hospital attention after using hand garden tools. The table shows, once again, just how often accidents in and around the home can happen, to anyone.

We won't go down the list item by item and explain how to avoid each and every possible pitfall. But there are certain things everyone should know about safely dealing with the appliances that are in most households. And there are also definite safety rules to be observed when using hand tools, electric power tools and gas-driven power tools and machines.

WATCH OUT FOR SHOCK

In chapter 2, there was a description of how electricity could cause a fire. Electricity can also kill or injure a person in another way. It can cause a severe or even fatal electric shock.

How many of you have taken a radio, a boom box, or similar appliance into the bathroom while you shower or bathe? No sense showering without some rock or rap. It can get you in the mood to go out. But it also can create a potentially fatal situation.

Water and electricity don't mix! A moderate electrical shock can turn fatal if you are standing in water. Even if just your hands are wet, the shock can become substantially worse. So don't bring an electrical appliance into the bathroom. It's all right if the radio or box runs on batteries, but not if you plug it into an electrical outlet.

The same basic rule applies in the kitchen. If you are washing dishes or have wet hands, don't fool with the toaster oven or blender, especially with the electric cord or plug.

A microwave oven can present a double threat. As with all appliances, a bad or frayed cord can shock you. And the microwaves themselves can be dangerous. Microwaves are electromagnetic waves that are absorbed by food as it cooks in a microwave oven. The energy in the waves agitates the molecules in the food. This agitation causes friction that causes the molecules to heat. Exposure to these waves can cause the same reaction to the molecules in human flesh.

Don't horse around near a microwave oven while it's in use. You might bump it and cause the door to open. Never open the door until the oven shuts off. And make sure that your parents or guardians have the microwave checked periodically for leaks. Never use any metal containers in the oven. Metal can reflect the waves and cause an electric current to jump from one surface to another inside the oven. It won't hurt you, but it will damage the oven, and may cause a fire. When you remove microwaved foods from the oven, be careful. The food is often very hot and can give off dangerous steam, which can cause painful burns.

As for other appliances, there is always the potential for a major electrical shock, especially if you try to experiment or play home repairman. Even young children can be fascinated by the inner workings of a television, radio, or clothes dryer. First of all, no one should ever take an electrical appliance apart without disconnecting the electrical plug.

Some appliances, such as televisions, can store electricity even after the plug is removed from the wall socket. So there is still a danger of a bad or fatal electrical shock after the set is unplugged. If you see someone in your family trying to repair a television, warn him. If you see friends playing with a discarded TV, tell them to back off. There can still be danger.

If you are using an appliance and feel a kind of tingle when you touch it, be careful. That means that electrical current is leaking somewhere. Unplug the appliance immediately and don't use it again until it is repaired. And if you see your younger brother or sister fooling around with an appliance that is plugged in, stop him or her immediately.

If there are infants or toddlers in your family, you can help to keep them safe by installing covers on all unused outlets. These inexpensive safety devices are available in some supermarkets and in many department stores. Remember, electrical outlets are right at eye level for a child who is crawling. Safety covers will prevent a curious child from poking his fingers into an outlet and getting a shock.

HAND AND POWER TOOLS

Nearly every house with a home workshop is equipped with a number of hand and power tools that are used to take care of

Infants love to explore, and may be especially curious about electrical outlets. Inexpensive safety covers on outlets can keep a young child from getting a shock.

repairs and other home projects like building shelves, paneling a room, or repairing a rotting deck. Unless there is adult supervision, children should not be found in a home workshop.

Hand tools such as chisels, knives, and even screwdrivers can cause bad cuts. Hammers can lead to painful bruises on the thumb and fingers. Any small piece of wood or metal can fly up and cause a serious or painful eye injury.

Nothing can stop the occasional accident in the home workshop. Even professional carpenters will miss with a hammer now and then, or slip with a chisel or handsaw.

There are, however, some important rules for keeping a workshop safe that everyone should follow:

1. Always wear eye protection, especially when hammering and cutting. A group called Prevent Blindness America says that close to half the 2.4 million people who have lost some vision because of an eye injury suffered the injury at home. Obviously, wearing safety goggles would prevent many of these injuries.
2. Use the right tool for the right job. Don't use a screwdriver when a chisel is called for. Don't use a pair of pliers as a hammer. Use the proper saw blade for whatever material is being cut.
3. Only use power tools after you have been taught the correct way to use them. Learn slowly, the same way a person would learn to drive a car. Make sure that whoever is teaching you watches you at first, to make sure you are using the tools correctly. Don't solo until he gives you permission. Power tool accidents can be very serious.
4. Never put your fingers near the blade of a power saw or similar cutting tool. Use a push stick to guide the wood past the blade. Never use your hand.
5. Make sure all cutting tools have sharp blades. A dull blade won't cut very well, but it sure can cut your hand or cause whatever you're cutting to jump up at you.
6. Many small projects, such as building model cars or planes, call for the use of a hot-glue gun. The glue is melted in the gun, flows onto the part that must be glued, then dries quickly. When using

If you are interested in working with tools, be sure to learn the proper way to use them from someone who knows.

a hot-glue gun, be careful. If the hot glue should flow onto your hand or arm, it can give you a bad burn. And the nozzle of the gun can burn you, too.
7. Keep all tools clean and in good working order. Check for fraying or cuts in electrical cords. A power tool can give the same kind of electrical shock as any other appliance.

There are many ways to learn about woodworking and fix-it projects. There are books available at libraries and bookstores, home repair and building shows on television, and shop courses on the use of tools at local schools.

Kids must learn the use of tools slowly and thoroughly. Never attempt a complicated project without consulting an adult. And never use a tool that is unfamiliar, especially power tools, without adult supervision. Realize that there are some projects you can do safely, and some you can't. Even adults sometimes must leave the more difficult projects to the pros.

LAWN AND GARDEN TOOLS AND MACHINERY

It's a hot summer day and you've got to cut the lawn. There has been a lot of rain lately, so the grass is high and soft. You slip on a pair of shorts but don't feel like putting on sneakers. It'll be cooler pushing that rotary mower in your bare feet.

For a while, everything goes fine. Then you start moving up and down a hill. The grass is still a little damp. You start down the hill again, thinking about a nice shower and a good dinner. What happens next happens so fast that you can't stop it. Suddenly, your feet slip and you fall down. One foot goes under the back end of the mower....

All it takes is one split second of carelessness and you could lose some or all of your toes or get a severe cut that requires a fast trip to the emergency room. This type of lawn mower accident is not at all uncommon. And just like many other accidents, it could have been prevented.

You should always be sure to wear sneakers or shoes when using a lawn mower. It's also better to wear jeans or other long pants, rather than shorts, to protect your legs from serious cuts that can result when the lawn mower kicks up rocks or twigs. And never mow directly up or down a hill. Mow hills from side to side. That way, if you do slip, there will be less chance that you will be injured by the lawn mower blade.

The blade is something to be avoided at all costs. *Never* reach into the grass chute to clear it while the mower is running. If you reach just a few inches too far, your fingers could get clipped. Always shut the mower down before cleaning the chute. And always use a stick or other object rather than your hand.

Ride-on mowers or lawn tractors also require caution. Never drive a tractor just for fun or for a joy ride. You should be taught very carefully how to drive and handle a tractor, just as if you were getting a license to drive a car. Let an adult work with you. Let him decide when you are ready to drive without supervision.

Tractors can turn over on hills and cause serious injuries. Like traditional mowers, they also have blade chutes that get clogged. Use the same rules that apply to rotary mowers when dealing with the blade. Remember, tractors are not meant to carry any passengers. Don't let a friend hop on the back for a quick ride. And *never* hop off to push if the tractor is spinning its wheels on a hill. Stop and think of the best solution. Usually, you can back down the hill carefully and find a better route.

Chain saws are another very dangerous yard tool. In fact, children should never use a chain saw at all. Too many bad things can happen. A loose chain can fly off and injure you. If you don't know how to cut wood correctly, the saw can kick back, shooting up from the log, and can catch you in the head or chest.

Chain saws are very dangerous tools and should be used only by people experienced in handling them. For this reason, we will not discuss any safety rules for handling a chain saw. Just don't use it.

Never use a lawn mower while barefoot. Wearing eye protection when you are doing yard work is a good idea, too.

Electric hedge clippers and nylon line edgers are not quite as dangerous as chain saws, but they still require careful handling. Several years ago, Bob Ojeda, a major league pitcher with the New York Mets, severely lacerated a finger on his pitching hand while using an electric hedge clipper. It definitely curtailed his career.

If you want to help with the yard work, ask your parents or guardians to teach you the correct way to hold and operate a hedge clipper. And if it's electric, always be aware of the electrical cord. If you cut it accidentally, you can get a severe or even fatal electrical shock.

Nylon line edgers cut grass and weeds by using a spinning nylon line, much like fishing line. Never use these tools in bare feet. The fast-moving nylon can inflict a severe cut. If you are using an electric edger, watch the cord. If you are using a gas operated edger, be careful when refueling it. As discussed earlier, gasoline is extremely flammable.

Another important rule that should not be overlooked when using any kind of mower, trimmer, or clipper, is always wear eye protection. All of these devices are capable of throwing particles of grass, stones, twigs, or other objects up at the eyes very quickly. A serious eye injury can result if you do not wear protection. This is as important while working in your yard as it is in your workshop!

Hand tools are not quite as dangerous as power tools. But you can be injured by shovels, rakes, and similar garden tools. Never plunge a sharp-edged shovel into the ground if someone else has his hands or feet close to where you are about to dig. And how many of you have been hit in the head with the handle after stepping on a rake that has been left on the ground teeth up?

Always take an extra second to watch out for others. Look where you are walking and working, and don't leave anything lying around that could injure someone else.

HOW TO HELP IF THERE IS AN ACCIDENT

In a perfect world, there would be no accidents. Home would be the safe haven most people would like it to be. But this is not a perfect world, and accidents will happen. Hopefully, as safety awareness increases, there will be fewer and fewer of them. But they will happen.

Since none of us knows beforehand what a new day will bring, we must be prepared. You know now that someday you or someone in your home might have a serious accident. If that happens, you can't panic. You need to be ready to help. That means not only knowing how to get professional help, but also knowing a few basic ways in which *you* can assist the victim before help arrives.

EMERGENCY NUMBERS

If someone in your home is badly injured, you must get professional help immediately. The fastest way to get help to your home is to use the telephone. If there is a 911 emergency number service in your area, it's easy. Just dial 911 and wait for an operator. Identify yourself. Tell the operator exactly where you live and the nature of the problem. That way, the 911 operator can get the right kind of help to you as quickly as possible.

If there is no 911 service where you live, then make sure the phone numbers for the police, fire department, ambulance, and poison control center are listed near *every* telephone in the house.

Make sure all the members of your family know how to use the phone to call for help. As soon as the youngest children are old enough to know their number, begin to teach them to use the phone. Lives have already been saved by children just old enough to talk and use the telephone.

Senior citizens who cannot get out of bed or up from a chair quickly should have a telephone within arm's reach. If that isn't possible, perhaps your parents or guardians will decide to install some kind of intercom system that can be used to alert other people in the house when help is needed.

SOME THINGS YOU CAN DO

No one expects you to be able to do what a medical professional can do. But you never know when you might be needed to help in an emergency until a doctor or emergency medical technician arrives. There are some basic first-aid procedures that every person should know. And it's recommended that at least one family member knows how to perform two major procedures—cardiopulmonary resuscitation (CPR) and the Heimlich maneuver.

CPR is used to restore breathing and heartbeat to victims of suffocation, drowning, electric shock, or medical emergencies such as heart attacks. CPR should be started immediately in cases of sudden unexpected death. CPR has literally brought many people back to life.

There are two phases of CPR that must be done in coordination with one another. The first is called mouth-to-mouth resuscitation, or rescue breathing. That means forcing your breath directly into the victim's mouth and down into the lungs. The second phase is a rhythmic compression of the chest above the heart.

The chest compressions are done between the rescue breaths. The compressions are given directly to the lower area of the sternum or breastbone, because it is a strong region of the chest. This area provides a stronger squeezing ability so the heart can be more easily manipulated. The compressions are done with the heel of one hand while the other hand is placed on top of the first to help apply pressure.

CPR techniques, however, are different for infants and small children than they are for adults. Done incorrectly, CPR can easily cause an injury to an infant or small child. Therefore, it is recommended that everyone learning CPR for both adults and children should do so by taking an approved course from a qualified instructor. That way, you'll be sure to know just the right way to do it.

For those who don't feel comfortable giving direct mouth-to-mouth resuscitation, there are two devices available that create a barrier between the rescuer and victim. They are a pocket mask and a rescue key. Both are made of plastic and cover the victim's mouth and nose. The rescuer can then give life-saving breaths without making direct contact with the victim's mouth.

Courses in cardiopulmonary resuscitation are given in most towns and cities. They are usually given by organizations such as the American Red Cross, American Heart Association, or perhaps by EMTs at your local firehouse or first-aid squad. Even ten- or twelve-year-old children can learn CPR.

The Heimlich maneuver is a way to clear the air passage of someone who is choking. Before this maneuver was developed, many people died after getting a piece of food or other object lodged in their throats.

Learning the Heimlich maneuver is not difficult. Ask your parents or guardians, or a teacher or scout leader to help you. Here are the simple steps that are involved:

- Get behind the person who is choking and wrap your arms around her waist. Make a fist with one hand and place the thumb side of the fist against the abdomen, slightly above the navel, but well below the tip of the breastbone.

You can make a difference in an emergency. Learning the Heimlich maneuver may help you to save the life of a friend or loved one.

- Then grasp your fist with your other hand and, using a quick inward and upward jerk, press into the abdomen. This should be continued until the victim spits out the object that is stuck in her throat. She will spit it out because you are forcing a rapid thrust of air up from the abdomen to push against the object from the inside.

Several notable people died from choking before the Heimlich maneuver was invented. They include bandleader Tommy Dorsey and World War II Admiral Richard L. Connelly. Among the many people whose lives were saved by this maneuver was former President Ronald Reagan.

OTHER THINGS YOU SHOULD KNOW

Here are a few important ways you can help an accident victim until professional medical help arrives at the scene of the emergency:

Falls—Make sure the victim is breathing, then call for help. Don't move her. This is especially true if you suspect a broken bone or a back or neck injury. Keep the victim warm until professional help arrives.

Bleeding—The bleeding from most cuts, even severe ones, can be stopped or slowed by direct hand pressure over the wound. Try to use a pad or clean cloth. Sterile gauze is best, but any clean, soft cloth will do. If blood soaks the cloth, don't remove it. Add more cloth on top and press more firmly with your hand.

A word of caution about helping someone who is bleeding. There are a number of dangers in exposing yourself to someone else's blood. Diseases such as AIDS and hepatitis, as well as a number of others, can be transmitted by tainted blood. In addition, germs on your hand can infect the person who is bleeding.

For these reasons, the American Red Cross recommends that people keep a barrier between blood and the hand. If you must put pressure on a bleeding wound and don't have safety gloves, you can use a plastic bag to cover your hand. You can even use tinfoil, anything that's available that the blood will not penetrate.

If there is nothing available in an extreme emergency and your hand does come into contact with someone's blood, wash it well in soap and water as quickly as possible. And tell a doctor or hospital official just what you did.

Head Injuries—If someone is hit in the head you must consider the severity of the injury. Obviously, if the person is unconscious, you must get help so the victim can be rushed to the hospital. If the victim seems alert and is walking and talking, then apply an ice pack to the point of impact. Any later sign of dizziness, vomiting, or confusion indicates that the victim should be taken to a doctor or hospital.

Burns—A simple burn from a match, a hot pipe or burst of steam is easy to treat. These small burns are called first degree burns. Pain can be relieved by applying cold water to the burned area or putting the burned area directly into cold water. Do not use ice cubes. Once the burn has completely cooled, a soothing ointment can be applied. Never apply ointment to anything but a *minor* burn. Never put butter on a burn.

Second degree burns, which penetrate to the second layer of skin and cause blistering and swelling, can also be treated with cold water. The skin should then be blotted dry and covered with a clean, dry dressing. If a large area is affected, the burns should be checked by a doctor.

Third degree burns go even deeper, destroying the skin all the way down to the muscles, bones, and even nerves. These burns should be considered an emergency. Call for help immediately.

Safety in the home is a full-time job. Everyone in the family should help, watching out for others as well as for themselves.

Perhaps the best advice is to focus on safety every day and work hard to eliminate the factors that cause accidents.

If an accident does happen, you've got to think fast and act quickly. Being prepared for any kind of emergency is a big part of the overall safety picture, too.

FURTHER READING

American Red Cross. *Standard First Aid.* St. Louis, Mo.: Mosby, 1993.

Anderson, Peggy K. *Safe at Home!* New York: Atheneum, 1992.

Carter, Sharon. *Coping With Medical Emergencies.* New York: Rosen, 1988.

Gay, Kathlyn, and Marjory Kline. *Silent Killers: Radon and Other Hazards.* New York: Watts, 1988.

Gutman, Bill. GO FOR IT! series: *Swimming.* New York: Marshall Cavendish, 1990.

Kusinitz, Marc. *Poison and Toxins.* New York: Chelsea House, 1992.

McGee, Eddie. *The Emergency Handbook.* New York: Simon and Schuster, 1985.

ORGANIZATIONS TO CONTACT

Gas Appliance Manufacturers Association
4 West Nebraska Street
Frankford, IL 60423
1-800-426-2811
(Call or write for a free consumer kit: "Hidden Hazards in Your Home." It includes a brochure and a video narrated by William Shatner.)

The Indoor Air Quality Information Clearinghouse
P.O. Box 37133
Washington, DC 20013-7133
1-800-438-4318
(This organization will answer questions and provide information about carbon monoxide, radon, asbestos, and formaldehyde.)

McDonald's Education Resource Center
3620 Swenson Avenue
P.O. Box 8002
St. Charles, IL 60174
1-800-627-7646
(A free education resource catalog is available. The catalog includes a family fire safety video, "Plan to Get Out Alive.")

National Fire Protection Association
P.O. Box 9146
Batterymarch Park
Quincy, MA 02269-9146
1-800-344-3555

National Rifle Association
11250 Waples Mill Road
Fairfax, VA 22030
1-800-231-0752
(Contact the NRA for information on safe gun handling.)

National Safe Kids Campaign
111 Michigan Ave. NW
Washington, DC 20010-2970
1-202-884-4993
(Send a stamped, self-addressed envelope for information about National Safe Kids Week events.)

National Safety Council
Customer Service
1121 Spring Lake Road
Itasca, IL 60143-3201
1-800-621-7619

U.S. Consumer Product Safety Commission
Office of Information and Public Affairs
Washington, DC 20207
1-800-638-2772

INDEX

ambulances, 43, 70
arson, 27

bleeding, 74
brush fires, 22
bunkbeds, 14, *15*
burns, 36, 38, 75

carbon monoxide detector, 44
carbon monoxide poisoning, 35, 38, 40–44, 45
cardiopulmonary resuscitation (CPR), 71–72
children's safety precautions
 electric shock, 62, *63*
 fire, 20, 33
 guns, *50*, 51, 52
 lead contamination, 45, 47
 poisons, 38, 45, 47
 on stairways, 13
 water safety, 53, 55, 56–57
 window guards, 13
choking, 71, 72, *73*, 74
cigarettes as cause of fires, 23, *24*, 25

drug overdoses, 35, 36, 38–40

electric shock, 9, 61–62, *63*, 66, 71
emergency numbers, 70–71
eye protection, 64, *68*, 69

false alarms, 27
fire, 8, *21*, 62
firebreaks, 22
fire department, 26, 27, 33, 70, 72
fire drills, 31, 33
fire extinguishers, 26, 29, 30–31
firefighters, 27, *32*, 33, 34
fireworks, 23, 25

guns. *See* children's safety precautions, guns.

hand tools, 62, 64, *65*, 66, 69
head injuries, 14, 18, 57–58, 75
heart attacks, 71
Heimlich maneuver, 71, 72, *73*, 74

kitchen hazards, 28–29

lawn mower accidents, 66–67, *68*
lead, 45, 46
lightning as cause of fire, 20, 22

National Rifle Association, 52
National Safety Council, 7, 8,
　16–17, 18, 35, 48–49, 53
911, 33, 70

poison control center, 42–43, 70
poisons, 8, 30, *37*, 48, 70

radon, 44–45, *46*

smoke detectors, 30, 31
socket, overloaded, 23, 26, 28
space heaters, 23, 26, 28
stairways, 10–11, *12*, 13
suffocation, 20, 71
swimming pools, *54*
swimming programs, 56–57

tractors, 67

water intoxication, 57
water safety, 53, 55, 56–57
window guards, 13

PHOTO CREDITS

Cover photo by David Young-Wolff/PhotoEdit; p. 6: Rob Gage/FPG International; p. 12: Mary Kate Denny/PhotoEdit; p. 15: Paul Rees/Tony Stone Worldwide; p. 21: Tony Freeman/PhotoEdit; p. 24: Gabe Palmer/The Stock Market; p. 32: Bob Llewelyn/Uniphoto; p. 37: Leinwand/Monkmeyer; pp. 42, 50, 65: David Young-Wolff/PhotoEdit; p. 46: Courtesy of the Rutgers University Eastern Regional Radon Testing Center; p. 52: Paul Howell/Gamma Liaison; p. 54: Yale/Monkmeyer; p. 56: Al Cook/Stock Boston; p. 63: Hiller/Monkmeyer; p. 68: Bob Daemmrich/Stock Boston; p. 73: Seth Resnick/Gamma Liaison.